SLOPPY KISSES

BY ELIZABETH WINTHROP
PICTURES BY ANNE BURGESS

MACMILLAN PUBLISHING CO., INC., NEW YORK

COLLIER MACMILLAN PUBLISHERS, LONDON

Macmillan Publishing Co., Inc.
866 Third Avenue, New York, N.Y. 10022
Collier Macmillan Canada, Ltd.
Printed in the United States of America

10   9   8   7   6   5   4   3   2   1

LIBRARY OF CONGRESS CATALOGING IN PUBLICATION DATA

Winthrop, Elizabeth.   Sloppy kisses.

SUMMARY: After her friend tells her kissing is for babies,
Emmy Lou tries to make do with a pat on the shoulder.
[1. Kissing—Fiction] I. Burgess, Anne. II. Title.
PZ7.W768Sl 1980 [E] 80-13673 ISBN 0-02-793210-9

8100234

To Papa

THE ORIGINAL SLOPPY KISSER

—E. W.

To my Aunt Lorena

—A. B.

Emmy Lou's family loved to kiss.
Mama kissed Papa good morning.
Papa kissed Dolly at breakfast.
Dolly kissed Mama good-bye
when she went to school.
Emmy Lou kissed Papa good-bye
when she went to school.
And when they came home,
it started all over again.
Emmy Lou's family just loved to kiss.

One day, when Papa dropped
Emmy Lou off at school,
Rosemary was standing on the steps,
watching them.
Papa gave Emmy Lou
a great big sloppy kiss.
"Good-bye, Emmy Lou," he said.
"Good-bye, Papa," Emmy Lou called.
"See you tonight."

"EEEE-YEW!" said Rosemary.
"Your father still kisses you?
  That's just for babies."
"It is?" asked Emmy Lou.
"Kissing is yukky," said Rosemary.
  And she went off to hang up her coat.
"It is?" Emmy Lou whispered.

All day long, Emmy Lou thought
about kisses.
That night when Papa came home,
he kissed Mama hello.
Then he kissed Dolly hello.
But when he tried to kiss Emmy Lou,
she turned her head away.
"I don't want you to kiss me any more,"
she said.
"Kissing is just for babies."

Papa looked at Mama.

"Kissing is for everybody," Papa said.

"Rosemary says kissing is yukky,"
  said Emmy Lou.

"I don't want you to kiss me any more."

"All right, Emmy Lou," said Mama.

"But we still love you."

That night Mama and Papa gave Emmy Lou
a little pat on the shoulder
when she went to bed.

Emmy Lou snuggled down under her covers.

It took her a long time to get to sleep.

The next day, whenever Papa tried
to kiss Emmy Lou, she shook her head.
"No, Papa," she said.
"No more sloppy kisses."
When Papa took Emmy Lou to school,
he just patted her on the top of her head
and walked away, looking very sad.
Rosemary was watching.
"I'm not letting them kiss me any more,"
Emmy Lou said proudly.
"I told them kissing is just for babies."
"That's right," said Rosemary.

Every night, when Mama and Papa
put Emmy Lou and Dolly to bed,
they would kiss Dolly good night,
and they would pat Emmy Lou
on the shoulder.

One night, Emmy Lou couldn't get to sleep.
She turned on one side and then the other.
She put her head under the pillow.
She pulled her blanket on
and pushed it off.
No matter what she did,
she could not get to sleep.

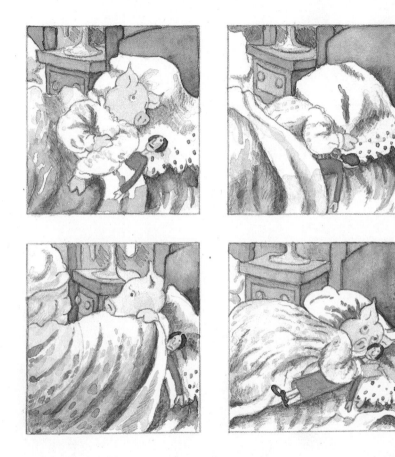

So she tiptoed into her parents' room.
"Mama," she said.
"I can't get to sleep."

"Do you want a
cup of juice?"
asked her mother.
"No," said Emmy Lou.

"Do you need
another blanket?"
asked her father.
"It's a little cool
tonight."
"No," said Emmy Lou.

"Would you like me to
read you a story?"
asked her mother.
"No," said Emmy Lou.

"I know
what you need,"
said her father.

He picked up Emmy Lou
and gave her a great big sloppy kiss.
Then he handed her to her mother,
who gave Emmy Lou a nice soft warm kiss.
Emmy Lou smiled.

They carried her back to bed
and tucked her in.
She fell right to sleep.

The next morning
Papa walked Emmy Lou to school.
Rosemary was standing on the steps.
Papa looked at Rosemary.
"Good-bye, Emmy Lou," he said.
He patted her on the shoulder
and started to walk away.

"Papa," Emmy Lou cried.
"Come back. You forgot to kiss me."
  She wrapped her arms around his neck
  and gave him a great big sloppy kiss.
"EEEE-YEW!" said Rosemary,
  just as Emmy Lou knew she would.
"Kissing is just for babies."

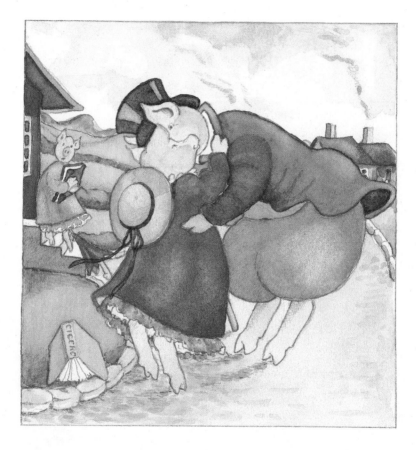

"It is not," said Emmy Lou.
"Kissing is for everybody."
And she gave Rosemary
a little kiss on the cheek
and walked inside.